Here Comes Summer!

by Peter Maloney
and Felicia Zekauskas

SCHOLASTIC INC.

New York   Toronto   London   Auckland   Sydney
Mexico City   New Delhi   Hong Kong   Buenos Aires

For Luke

ISBN 0-439-55363-6

12 11 10 9 8 7 6   6 7 8 9/0

Printed in the U.S.A.
First printing, May 2004

CHAPTER 1
End of the Year

It was June.
School was ending soon.

Mrs. Robinson asked the children what they were going to do for their summer vacations.

"I'm going to visit my grandparents
for the summer," said Felicia.

"I'm going to
the beach,"
said Cliff.

"I'm going to
a lake," said Tobi.

"And I'm going to the moon!"
shouted Russ Deluca.

Everybody laughed except for Peter.
Peter didn't want summer to come.

CHAPTER 2
Peter Takes a Trip

Peter and Felicia were walking
home from school.
"I wish school wouldn't end,"
said Peter.

"But you had lots of fun last summer,"
said Felicia.

"That was before school started,"
said Peter. "Before I met you
and Tobi and Rich and Lew
and Patty and Cliff and . . ."

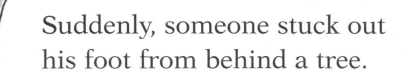

Suddenly, someone stuck out
his foot from behind a tree.

Peter fell.
Felicia gasped.
Russ Deluca laughed.
"And don't forget me!"
he said.

Felicia helped Peter up.

"I'm going to miss everybody this summer," said Peter. "Except, maybe, Russ Deluca."

CHAPTER 3

Class Cleanup

The next day, the class began its
year-end cleanup.
"We've got a lot of things to throw out
or take home," said Mrs. Robinson.

The children went through their desks.
They found some interesting things.

Tobi found a picture of a pumpkin.
"I drew this in October," she said.

Rich held up a
drawing of a turkey.
"I did this in November!" he said.

"I got these in February," said Felicia, holding up a handful of Valentine's Day cards.

Russ Deluca held up a piece of
bubble gum.
"I chewed this back in April," he said.

"Look what I found!" said Peter.
It was a story about Peter's vacation
last summer.

"Wow!" said Mrs. Robinson. "You did that last September — almost a whole year ago."

There were drawings of Peter in the pool, in the park, and at the zoo.

"It looks like you had a lot of fun
last summer," said Mrs. Robinson.

"I guess I did," said Peter.

CHAPTER 4
The Last Day

The next day was the last day of
school.

"Who hasn't told us their summer
plans yet?" asked Mrs. Robinson.

Rich, Patty, Peter, and Felicia all raised their hands.

"I'm going to camp to learn the violin," said Rich.

"I'm going to take swimming lessons," said Patty.

"And I'm doing exactly what I did last summer," said Peter.

"And I'm going to spend my vacation playing with Peter," said Felicia. "He really knows how to make summer fun!"

"But I thought you were going to spend the summer at your grandparents' house," said Peter.

"I was," said Felicia. "Until I talked
them into visiting *me* instead!"

CHAPTER 5
School's Out

The bell was about to ring.
The school year was about to end.
Everybody was laughing and smiling,
except for Russ Deluca.
Russ looked sad.

"What's wrong, Russell?" asked Mrs.
Robinson.

"I'm going to miss everybody," said
Russ.

Mrs. Robinson gave Russ a pat on the back.
"Don't worry, everybody's going to miss you, too," said Mrs. Robinson.

"Well, almost everybody,"
laughed Peter and Felicia.